MW01132759

THE
Solar
System

BY MARION DANE BAUER
ILLUSTRATED BY JOHN WALLACE

Ready-to-Read

Simon Spotlight
New York London Toronto Sydney New Delhi

For Barbara Hill,
the Sun in my world
—M. D. B.

For Eli
—J. W.

SIMON SPOTLIGHT

An imprint of Simon & Schuster Children's Publishing Division
1230 Avenue of the Americas, New York, New York 10020
This Simon Spotlight paperback edition August 2024
Text copyright © 2024 by Marion Dane Bauer
Illustrations copyright © 2024 by John Wallace
SIMON SPOTLIGHT, READY-TO-READ, and colophon are registered
trademarks of Simon & Schuster, LLC.
Simon & Schuster: Celebrating 100 Years of Publishing in 2024
For information about special discounts for bulk purchases, please contact
Simon & Schuster Special Sales at 1-866-506-1949 or
business@simonandschuster.com.
Manufactured in the United States of America 0724 LAK
2 4 6 8 10 9 7 5 3 1
Library of Congress Cataloging-in-Publication Data
Names: Bauer, Marion Dane, author. | Wallace, John, 1966– illustrator. |
Bauer, Marion Dane. Our universe.
Title: The solar system / by Marion Dane Bauer ; illustrated by John
Wallace. Description: New York, New York : Simon Spotlight, [2024] |
Series: Our universe | "Ready-to-read." | Summary: "There is so much to
explore in our solar system. Learn all about the planets, moons, asteroids,
and more that orbit our star, the Sun"— Provided by publisher.
Identifiers: LCCN 2023048525 (print) | LCCN 2023048526 (ebook) |
ISBN 9781665958431 (hardcover) | ISBN 9781665958424 (paperback) |
ISBN 9781665958448 (ebook) Subjects: LCSH: Solar system—Juvenile
literature. Classification: LCC QB501.3 .B38 2024 (print) | LCC QB501.3
(ebook) | DDC 523.2—dc23/eng/20231122 LC record available at
https://lccn.loc.gov/2023048525 LC ebook record available at
https://lccn.loc.gov/2023048526

Glossary

✦ **asteroids** (say: A-stuh-royds): small, rocky bodies found in space.

✦ **axis** (say: AK-suss): an imaginary straight line about which a geometric body rotates.

✦ **comets** (say: KAH-mutts): space objects made of ice that often have long tails made of gas and dust.

✦ **dwarf planets** (say: DWORF PLA-nuhts): space objects that circle the Sun but do not shift other objects from their orbit.

✦ **gas giant** (say: GAS JIE-unt): a large planet composed of gas surrounding a solid core.

✦ **ice giant** (say: IESS JIE-unt): a large planet composed of icy materials surrounding a rocky core.

✦ **meteoroids** (say: MEE-tee-uh-royds): space rocks that range in size from grains to small asteroids.

✦ **objects** (say: AWB-jekts): material things that can be observed.

✦ **orbit** (say: OR-buht): to move in a circle around another object.

Note to readers: Some of these words may have more than one definition. The definitions above match how these words are used in this book.

Do you know what
is at the center of
our solar system?
Our shining Sun!

Eight planets,
several **dwarf planets**, and
over a million **asteroids**
all **orbit** the Sun.

These **objects**, along with **comets**, **meteoroids**, moons, dust, and gases, make up our solar system.

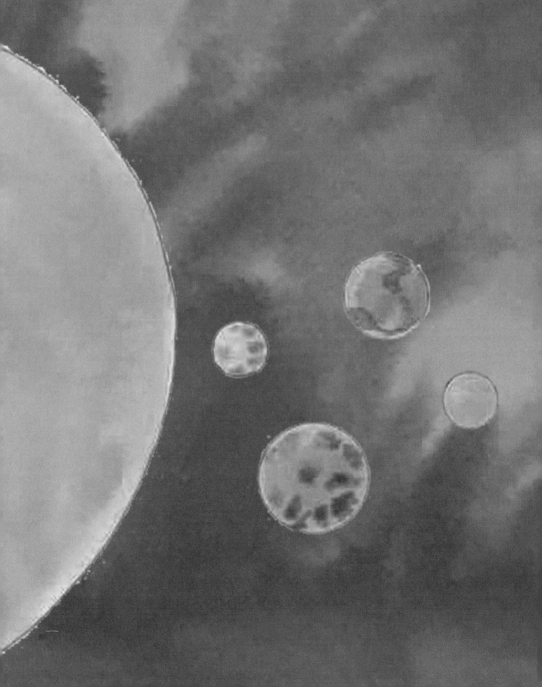

Mercury lies closest
to the Sun.

It is the smallest planet.
It is the fastest, too.
Mercury circles the Sun
every eighty-eight days.

Next comes Venus,
the hottest planet.

You can see Venus in
the sky just before sunrise
and just after sunset.

Earth is the only planet
known to support life.
Our Earth supports
every kind of life.

Giraffes and mushrooms,
butterflies and sharks,
giant redwood trees.

And us.

Mars is the last
of the rocky planets.

People have long talked
about living on Mars,
but the air is toxic, and
it gets very, very cold.

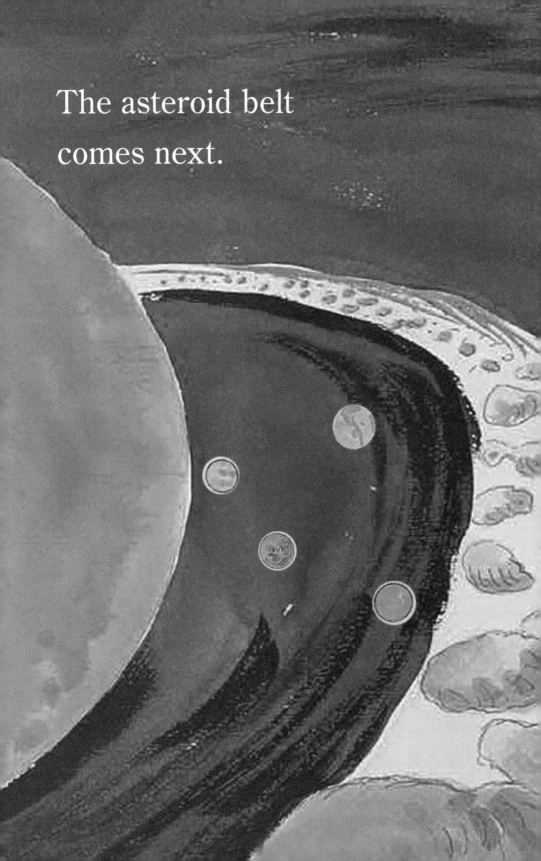

The asteroid belt
comes next.

It is made up of dust
and rocks traveling
around the Sun.

Jupiter is
a **gas giant**.
More than one
thousand Earths
could fit inside
Jupiter!

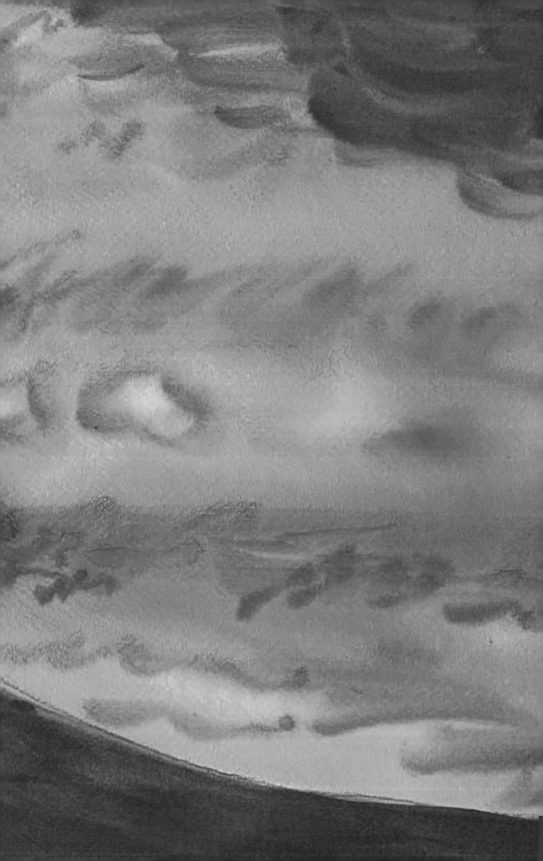

Saturn, another gas giant,
is famous for its shining rings.

The rings are made up
of ice, rocks, and dust.

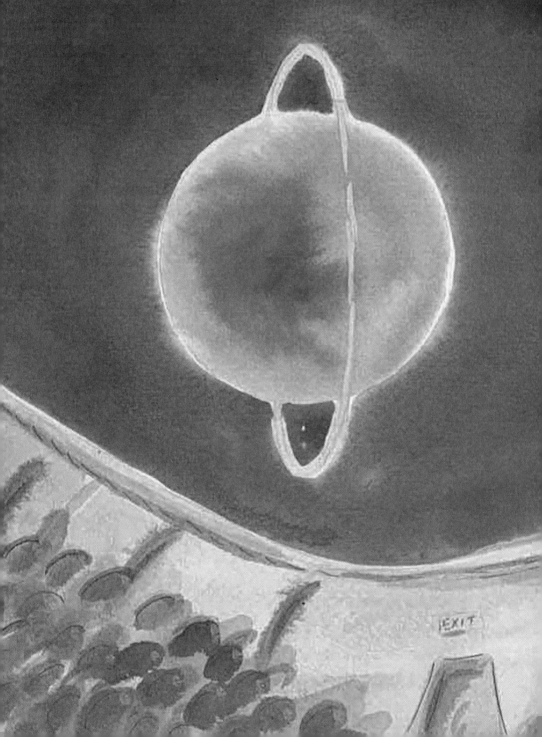

Uranus is an **ice giant**.

Uranus appears to spin on its side because of its tilted **axis**.

Neptune, another ice
giant, is so far from
the Sun that each orbit
takes almost 165 Earth years.

165 Years Ago

Today

Beyond Neptune,
dwarf planets like Pluto
and hundreds of thousands
of frozen objects
circle the Sun.

And beyond that . . .

are wonders
yet to be discovered!

Interesting Facts

✦ Our solar system is part of a galaxy called the Milky Way. Our Sun is one of a hundred billion stars in the Milky Way.

✦ Scientists classify the Sun as a yellow dwarf star.

✦ Gravity keeps the planets—and everything else—circling the Sun.

✦ The Sun is so big, more than one million Earths could fit inside it. It makes up 99.8 percent of the mass of our solar system.

✦ Each journey of the Earth around the Sun makes a year. Each rotation of our planet makes a day and a night.

✦ You could not walk on Jupiter, Saturn, Uranus, or Neptune. Their surfaces are not solid. In fact, they are made up of gases.

✦ Much of the time, Saturn is the most distant planet you can see without a telescope.

✦ Earth is in what scientists call the Goldilocks zone—not too hot, not too cold. The temperature is just right for water to be liquid.

✦ Scientists think that farther out than we can see, a Planet X might exist, ten times larger than Earth and about twenty times farther from the Sun than Neptune.

✦ Most of our solar system is empty space.